BOOK OF POWER

Welcome to the world of
MASK
MOBILE ARMOURED STRIKE KOMMAND

Imagine a world where there is more to reality than meets the eye. Where illusion and deception team up with man and machine to create a world of sophisticated vehicles and weaponry, manned by agents and counter-agents.

Book of Power

The MASK mission: to protect a mystical book and its secret power from the evil of VENOM's grasp. Matt Trakker and his team of brave agents fearlessly confront the danger, while Scott and his friend T-Bob assist in their *own* special way.

The fourth gripping **MASK** adventure.

MATT TRAKKER – SPECTRUM

MATT TRAKKER – ULTRA FLASH

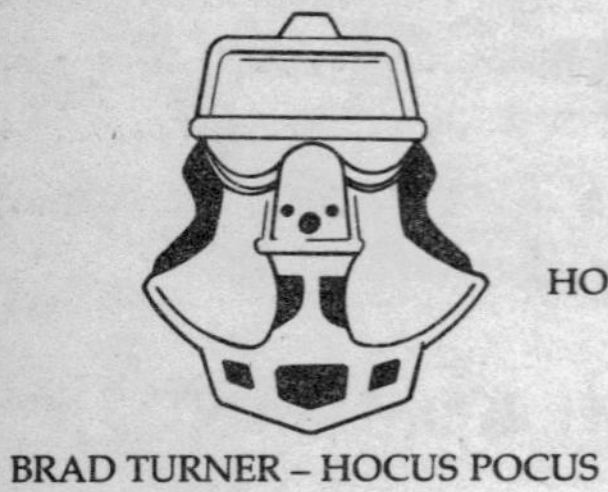

HONDO MACLEAN – BLASTER

BUDDIE HAWKES – PENETRATOR

BRAD TURNER – HOCUS POCUS

BRUCE SATO – LIFTER

DUSTY HAYES – BACKLASH

ALEX SECTOR – JACKRABBIT

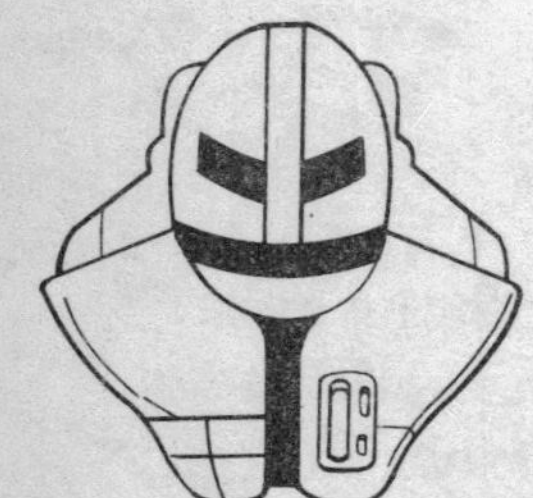

CLIFF DAGGER – THE TORCH

SLY RAX – STILETTO

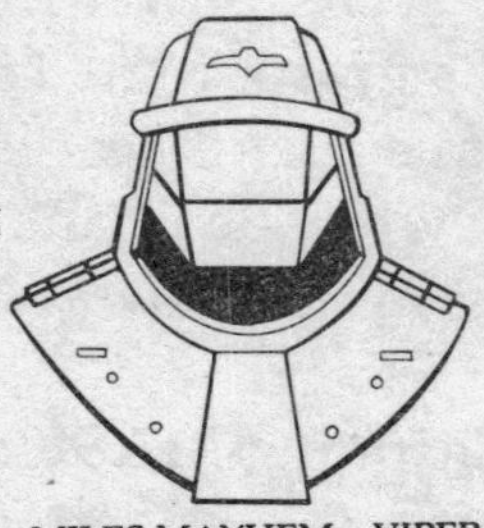

MILES MAYHEM – VIPER

MASK

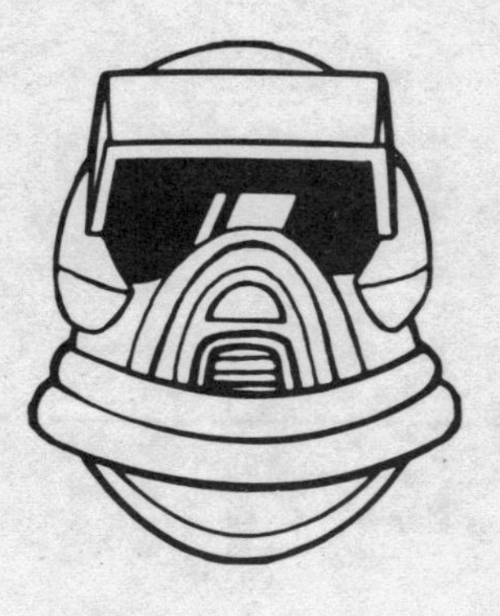

BOOK OF POWER

novelisation by
Kenneth Harper

Illustrated by Bruce Hogarth

KNIGHT BOOKS
Hodder and Stoughton

First published by Knight Books 1986
Second impression 1986

British Library C.I.P.
Harper, Kenneth
Book of power.–(MASK; 4)
I. Title II. Series
823'.914[J] PZ7

ISBN 0-340-39977-5

The characters and situations in this book are entirely imaginary and bear no relation to any real person or actual happening

Printed and bound in Great Britain for
Hodder and Stoughton Paperbacks, a
division of Hodder and Stoughton Ltd.,
Mill Road, Dunton Green, Sevenoaks,
Kent (Editorial Office: 47 Bedford
Square, London, WC1B 3DP) by
Cox & Wyman Ltd., Reading.
Photoset by Rowland Phototypesetting Ltd.,
Bury St Edmunds, Suffolk

ONE

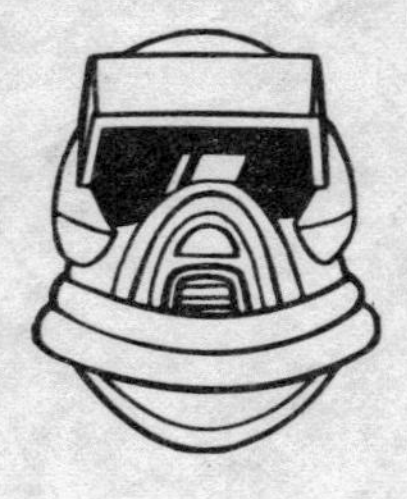

The shop stood in a quiet side-street. It sold curious, occult books and general bric-a-brac. On display in the window were stone carvings, pieces of ancient jewellery and weird objects in dark wood. There was a mystic air about the whole place and it attracted few visitors. The atmosphere inside was cold and unsettling.

In a sealed vault beneath the premises, a strange ritual was taking place. With his hood concealing his features, a monk was chanting in a long-dead language. Against the wall was a crude altar that was surmounted by a huge, ugly, expressionless stone face. The monk held a staff and the same face was carved on that as well.

There was a third version of the face.

On the Book of Power!

The volume was protected by a magnificent glass cabinet. It was a large, thick, leatherbound book with a metal clasp holding it shut. Seen in the flickering light of the torches that burned on the walls, the book seemed to glow and exude a fierce energy. The face on its front cover was evil and frightening.

The monk completed his incantations then bowed in front of the glass cabinet. He spoke with the utmost reverence.

'Blessed Book of Power! Reveal to us the way. Holder of Ancient Secrets. Guide us with your wisdom.'

The man was so preoccupied with his ritual that he did not hear the noises from upstairs. Dark shadows had fallen across the interior of the deserted shop then heavy footsteps crossed the floor. Three sturdy figures descended the stone steps that led to the cellar. They were soon confronted by a stout metal door.

Behind the door, the monk continued to implore.

'Book of Power! Come to our aid.'

CRASH!!!!

The door to the vault was blown off its hinges.

Startled by the blast, the monk swung round and cringed in terror when he saw the three menacing figures standing there. The first was wearing his distinctive Viper mask that could spit corrosive poison. He was leader of an organisation dedicated to evil.

It was Miles Mayhem. Head of VENOM – Vicious Evil Network of Mayhem.

Behind him were his two main henchmen, Cliff Dagger and Sly Rax, big, brutal characters who would stop at nothing to achieve their ends. Dagger was wearing his Torch mask while Rax was hidden beneath his Stiletto mask.

Mayhem's voice echoed around the chamber.

'The Book of Power. I want it.'

The monk tried desperately to shield the glass cabinet.

'There is no Book of Power,' he protested, nervously

'Give it to me!' ordered Mayhem.

'But it does not exist.'

'Out of my way.'

Mayhem grabbed the monk and hurled him viciously against a wall. Hurt by the impact, the man pointed a boney finger at his cruel adversary and gestured with his staff.

'The curses of the ages upon you!'

'Shut him up, Rax,' commanded Mayhem.

'My pleasure,' grunted Sly Rax, turning to face the hapless monk. 'Stiletto – fire!'

The mask obeyed and half a dozen stiletto knives shot from it to pin the monk to the wall. He tried to get free but the long blades held his robes securely.

Miles Mayhem gazed in delight at the Book of Power. Behind his mask, he gave a sinister smile and let out a low cackle of triumph.

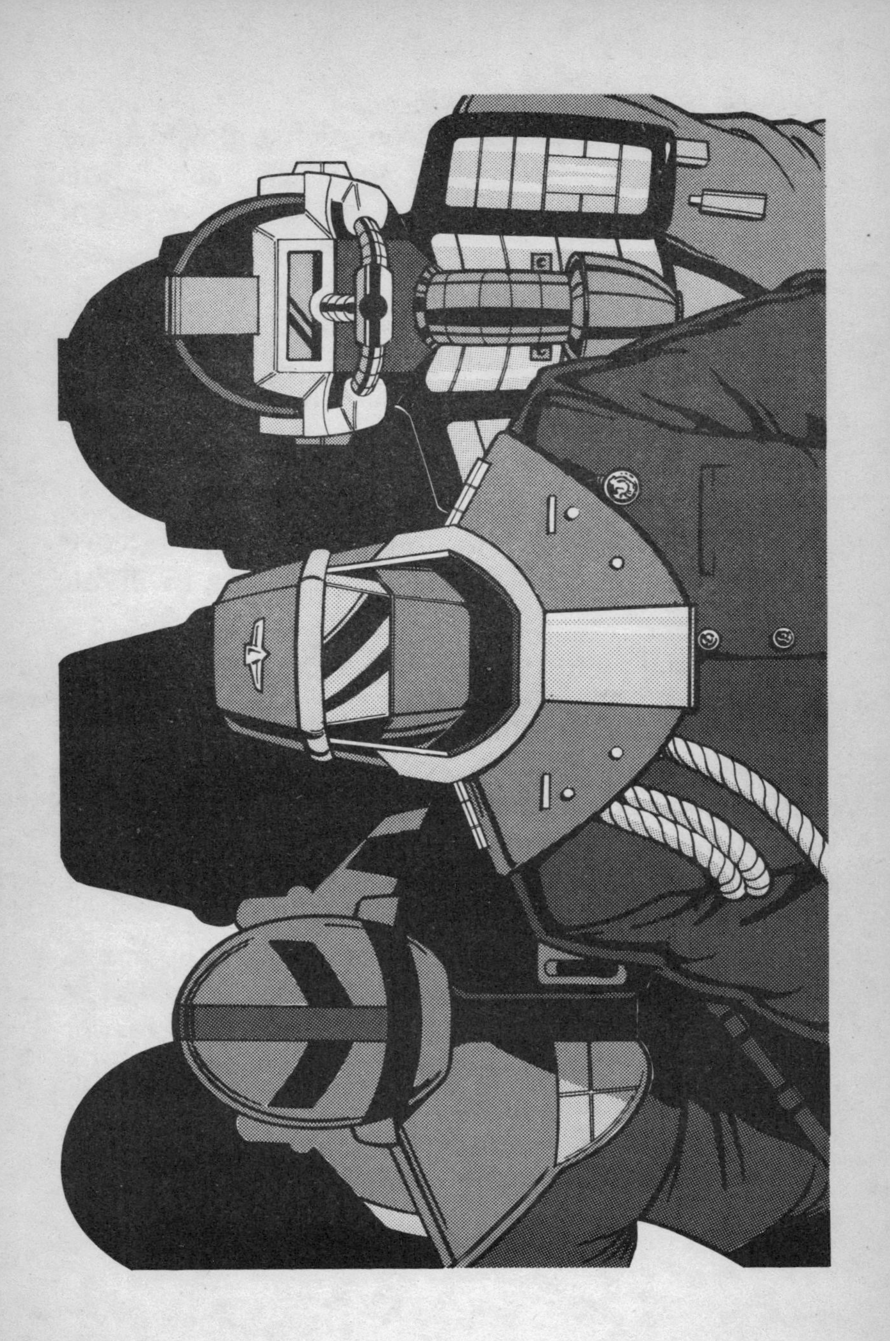

'Now for the final stroke!'

He bunched a fist and brought his gloved hand down with such force that the glass cabinet was smashed to smithereens. Tiny shards of glass went everywhere.

'No!' yelled the monk. 'Don't touch it.'

But his anguished cries were in vain.

Mayhem reached out to pick up the treasured volume. Lifting it from its place, he held it aloft in celebration.

'At last! The Book of Power is mine!'

'It can never be truly yours,' warned the monk.

'Nothing can stop me now,' added the VENOM leader. 'This Book will make me invincible. I will rule the world.'

'With us to help you,' noted Sly Rax.

'Yeah,' agreed Cliff Dagger.

The three of them shared a laugh then Mayhem took control.

'We must get away at once.'

'Our combat vehicles are ready,' said Rax.

'Then let's get back to them.'

They moved quickly to the door.

'You won't get away with this!' insisted the monk.

'We already have,' sneered Mayhem.

'Nice doing business with you,' teased Dagger.

'Sure,' said Rax with a snigger. 'I always wanted to get my knife into a monk.'

'Let's go!' decided Mayhem.

And he led his henchmen out at a brisk trot.

The monk struggled but he was held in position like a gigantic butterfly that has been pinned by its wings. His loud wail pursued them up the cellar steps.

'Bring the Book of Power back – or you are doomed!'

Above the altar, the stone face darkened with anger.

Dusty Hayes drove along happily in his jeep as he went on his delivery rounds. He was a renowned pizza cook and his talents made him very popular. There were always dozens of orders for his delicious pizzas. What none of his many customers knew, however, was the fact that Dusty was also a MASK agent – one of the small, fearless band of men who had been trained to fight against the forces of evil.

A wild, fun-loving, crazy cowboy, Dusty had a devil-may-care attitude towards life. His colleagues all acknowledged that the former stunt man was the best driver in the MASK team.

He needed all his driving skills now.

As Dusty brought the jeep up to an intersection, two vehicles shot past him so close that he had to swerve out of their way. The pizza boxes that were stacked up on the seats were thrown to the floor. Dusty was about to wave a fist after the departing machines, when he recognised them.

Jackhammer and Piranha. Two VENOM vehicles.

'Well, bust my britches! Those VENOM varmints!'

At this moment, the monk, who had finally torn himself free from the knives, came bounding out of the shop, shouting at the top of his voice.

'Thieves! They stole my book.'
'What book?' asked the MASK agent.
'It's priceless.'
'Why, pardner?'
'Someone stop them!'
Dusty spun his jeep around in a flash.
'I'll head 'em off at the pass!'
With a roar of his engine, he gave chase at once.
The monk watched him and began to chant once more in the ancient language. He knew that the theft of the Book of Power was much more than a casual act of robbery.
It was a disaster.

Miles Mayhem sat in the passenger seat of Jackhammer while Cliff Dagger drove the machine. Both had removed their masks now. Mayhem's stern face had the mark of authority to it. His big moustache bristled with pleasure as he examined the Book of Power, running his hands all over it.
'We did it!'
'Yeah,' said Dagger.
'This book will lead us to an ancient city of riches and an idol worth millions.'
'Good.'
'I'm going to make sure it never gets out of my reach.'
'Are you going to chain it to yourself?'
'No, you idiot. I'm going to use this tracking device.'
'Ah. That's clever.'

'Everything I do is clever.'

'Except employing me.'

Dagger grinned at his own joke but Mayhem had not heard. He was too busy inserting the minute device into the spine of the book. The bug gave off electronic signals that he would be able to monitor.

'With so much at stake, we can't be too careful.'

'No, boss.'

The VENOM machine powered its way on, followed by Sly Rax on Piranha, the motorcycle and sidecar that could convert to a submarine. Trailing them from a discreet distance was Dusty Hayes in his jeep.

All three vehicles left the city limits and drove on into rocky country. Mountains soon towered on all sides of them. Clouds of dust were sent up from their spinning wheels.

Dagger was still smirking about their success when he noticed something up ahead of them. It wiped the grin off his face immediately. Standing near the side of the road was the monk whom they had left pinned to the wall back in the vault. Or so Dagger thought. He did not realise that it was a different man in the same robes and hood.

'Hey!' he exclaimed. 'It's that monk from the shop.'

'How did *he* get here?' wondered Mayhem.

'Magic.'

'I don't like the look of this.'

The VENOM vehicles went past the monk and raced around a bend. They were greeted by a sight that astounded them even more. The monk was now standing on the top of a mountain near some large boulders. Once again, they were fooled by an optical illusion. It was a different man from the one who had been waiting beside the road. Like his two colleagues, the third monk wore identical apparel and he too held a staff which bore the carved face on it.

'There he is again!' said Dagger.

'I don't believe it!' snarled Mayhem.

'He's playing games with us, boss.'

The monk waved his staff with the frightening face.

'Stop!' he decreed. 'Return the Book of Power!'

'Never!' howled Mayhem.

'This is your last chance!'

'Out of my way!'

Seeing that the vehicles were not going to stop, the monk waved his staff in the air. There was a thunderous roar as the boulders began to roll down the mountainside. With gathering momentum, they tumbled faster and faster, bringing a whole flurry of rocks and smaller stones in their wake. The noise became deafening.

Mayhem, Dagger and Rax were struck dumb.

Danger threatened to engulf them.

They were now in the path of an avalanche.

TWO

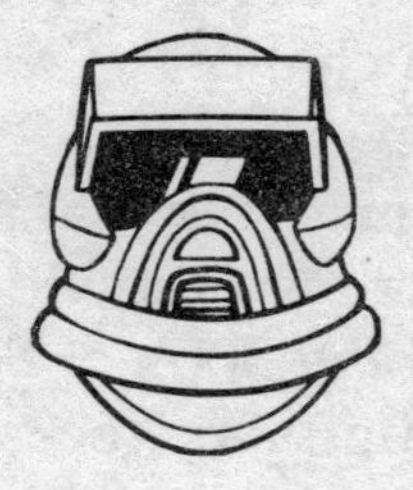

As soon as he saw the rockslide up ahead, Dusty Hayes took prompt action. Jamming his foot down hard on the brake, he swung on the driving wheel and took the jeep around in a half-circle. Thanks to the speed of his reflexes and his expert control of the machine, he stopped just short of the falling boulders. He gave a wry grin.

'Ain't no way through those hailstones.'

The VENOM vehicles decided otherwise.

They were trying to outrun the avalanche. With rocks starting to fill up the narrow canyon, they accelerated madly in the hope of making it to the other end. It was a hopeless task. Boulders began to crash on to the road all round them.

Cliff Dagger found his voice again.

'He-e-e-e-lp!'

'Keep driving!' urged Mayhem.

'This is worse than rush hour on the freeway!'

'Watch that rock!'

Dagger dodged one rock but took a glancing blow from another.

'Be more careful!' ordered Mayhem.

'We haven't got a chance.'

'Shut up and keep going!'

'Why didn't you just give that monk the book?'

'*Nothing* will make me part with this.'

Mayhem gripped the Book of Power to his chest as the ride got even bumpier. Rocks and stones littered the road now and they had no choice but to go straight over them.

Dagger was not enjoying his roller-coaster ride.

'Yiiiiiii!'

'Whoah!' yelled Mayhem.

'I'm scared!' admitted Dagger.

'Nonsense!'

'It's not nonsense.'

'A VENOM agent is never afraid,' insisted his leader.

'Well, this one is!'

And he had good reason to be.

At that moment, several more boulders came bouncing down the mountainside to hit the vehicle. It was completely out of control and went into a dizzy spin. All they could do was to hang on. The impact

was so great that the Book of Power was knocked out of Mayhem's hands.

'Come back!' he roared.

But the book flew out of the window and sailed through the air. Another boulder then came out of nowhere and struck the book with full force, sending it on a long journey down the canyon.

Dusty Hayes was speeding away from the danger when the missile hurtled past him to land on the ground. The metal clasp glinted in the sun and the skull-like carving caught his attention. He brought the jeep to a juddering halt and reached down to scoop up the book.

'Got'cha!'

He studied it with fascination. It was quite unlike any book he had ever seen. Apart from being very heavy, it had peculiar markings all over its cover. Flicking back the clasp, he opened it up. Strange, mystic music played and the page glowed in front of his eyes.

Dusty snapped it shut in alarm.

'I only ever read paperbacks.'

Putting the book among the pizza boxes on the rear seat, he set off again hell for leather. He knew instinctively that the volume had some uncanny power. It was a case for MASK to handle.

'I'd better get this to Matt!' he told himself.

While Dusty raced off in the jeep, the VENOM vehicles had come to a dead halt. Both of them were caught up in the avalanche and half-covered by rocks.

Cliff Dagger spat out a mouthful of gravel.

'What do we do now?'

'We've got to get the book!' announced Mayhem.

'How?'

'The bug will lead us to it.'

'But we're trapped under these rocks.'

'Then dig us out.'

'With my bare hands?'

'Bare hands, bare feet – anything! Now get busy!'

Dagger pushed the first few rocks away. He knew how vital it was to recapture the Book of Power. It made him work all the harder.

The Trakker mansion was a vast, gracious dwelling set in its own grounds. It was the home of a multi-millionaire and it lacked nothing. At the rear of the mansion were expansive green lawns with well cut grass.

Two small figures stood in the middle of a lawn.

'Okay, T-Bob. Pass the football.'

'Do the what?'

'Pass the football.'

Scott Trakker was an intelligent, lively young boy with a talent for creating mischief. T-Bob, his friend and constant companion, was a short, egg-shaped robot whose full name of Thingamebob had been shortened for convenience. Normally, T-Bob had no trouble understanding what he was told but Scott was finding it difficult to teach the robot the basic rules of American football.

'Pass the football!' he repeated.
'How do I do that?' asked T-Bob.
'I taught you how *yesterday*.'
'Yesterday?'
'The day before today.'
'Funny,' said T-Bob, scratching his metallic head. 'I don't remember a thing. Guess one of my chips must be defective.'
He opened a panel in his chest and put a hand in.
'What are you doing?' wondered Scott.
'Just checking.' The robot pulled out a couple of silicon chips. 'Let's see . . . My potato chip is fine. So's my chocolate cookie chip . . .'
He popped them into his mouth and swallowed them.
'Just *throw* the football,' urged Scott, impatiently.
'Throw it or pass it?'
'Comes to the same thing.'
'Why didn't you *say* so?'
T-Bob wound up his arm like a baseball pitcher then bounced the ball on the grass as if it were a basketball. Aiming it at Scott, he then unleashed it with such velocity that it went straight through the boy's hands and exploded against the nearest wall.
'Oops!' T-Bob covered his eyes.
Scott heaved a deep sigh.
'Back to the drawingboard!'

At the front of the house, meanwhile, Matt Trakker was in the process of seeing off a guest. Mr Davidson was a smartly-dressed art expert who had come to collect a painting that was being donated to a public gallery. He was very grateful to the generous millionaire. He put the painting into his car then turned to shake Matt's hand.

'Thank you, Mr Trakker.'

'My pleasure.'

'This will make a tasteful addition to the exhibition.'

'Only too glad to be of help, Mr Davidson.'

Before the visitor could take his farewell, there was a loud roar and Dusty Hayes came haring towards them in his jeep. Slamming on his brakes, he brought the vehicle to a halt beside Mr Davidson's car. In sending up a cloud of dirt, Dusty had made the other machine dusty as well.

Scott and T-Bob heard the jeep from behind the house and they came around the angle of the building to investigate. The boy was surprised to see the new arrival.

'Dusty! Wonder what he's doing here?'

'As long as he hasn't come to pass the football,' said T-Bob.

'Let's just listen.'

Dusty was panting with the excitement of his news.

'You won't believe what I've got, Matt!'

'Oh?'

He heard the warning in Matt's voice and noticed Mr Davidson. The art expert thought he was calling on a philanthropist. He had no idea that Matt Trakker was also the mastermind behind MASK. Dusty knew that he must not reveal this fact to anyone outside the organisation.

'Yeah,' he said. 'It's a pepperoni pizza . . . *special* pepperoni. Just like you ordered, sir.'

Instead of handing the Book of Power over, he slipped it into a large pizza box to disguise it. He offered it to Matt who took it from him with a smile of understanding.

'With lots of cheese,' promised Dusty.

'That's the way I like 'em,' conceded Matt.

Mr Davidson got into his limousine and looked out.

'Thank you again, Mr Trakker.'

'Find a good place to hang that painting.'

'We will, don't worry. Goodbye.'

'Be seeing you.'

The limousine drew away and rolled off down the drive. Matt Trakker was able to concentrate on the box in his hand. He looked at it in some consternation.

'VENOM really wanted that.'

'A *pizza*?'

'Nope. *This*.'

He opened the box to display the Book of Power. Matt was impressed and intrigued. Dusty opened the book and the strange music played again. The page was bathed in a bright glow.

'Ever read a book like that before, Matt?'

'No,' confessed the other.

'It's kinda weird.'

Matt closed the book and pulled down the cover of the box.

'If VENOM were after this, it must be important.'

'Important enough for them to steal it from some poor old monk, anyway. They grabbed it from this strange shop.'

'We'd better check this out.'

'The computer?'

'Yes. We'll take the Bullet Shuttle.'

'That's what I call a *real* pony express.'

'Let's go into the house.'

The mansion was connected to MASK headquarters by a long tube-like corridor down which the Bullet Shuttle travelled at high speed. As the two agents went into the building on their way to the computer room, Scott Trakker came forward with T-Bob.

'Did you see that?' demanded the boy.

'See what?'

'It's so selfish. Keeping all that pizza for themselves.'

'Maybe they're hungry.'

'*I'm* hungry as well,' argued the boy.

'You're always hungry.'

'I want a slice of that pizza.'

'Too late. It's gone.'

'Only as far as the computer room. We'll follow it.'

'We can't,' complained T-Bob. 'The computer room is out of bounds to us. Your Dad says we're not allowed in there.'

'He won't know anything about it.'

'I'm against the idea, Scott.'

'Too bad. I'm going after that pizza.'

'Is it worth it?'

'Of course. You heard Dusty. It's pepperoni.'

'With lots of cheese.'

'My favourite!'

Laughing to himself, Scott led the way into the mansion.

He thought he was on the trail of some food but the pizza box contained something altogether more dangerous. If the boy had known what was going to happen, he would never have gone to the computer room. The Book of Power held dark secrets.

Scott Trakker would soon learn what they were.

THREE

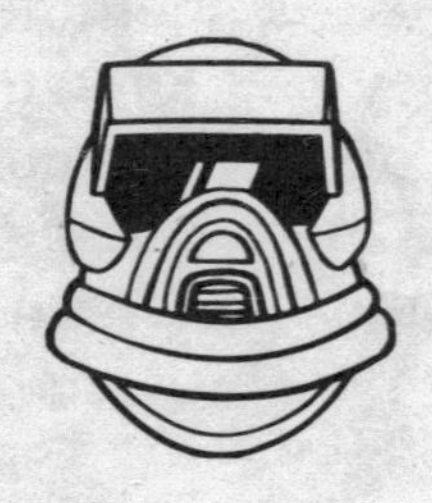

The computer room was packed with high technology. Banks of sophisticated equipment stood everywhere and there was a faint electronic hum. Matt Trakker brought Dusty Hayes into the room and they crossed to the main console. The Book of Power looked decidedly out of place. It was a relic of an old world thrust into a new one, an ancient tome in an ultra-modern setting. The carved head on the front cover seemed displeased.

Matt scrutinised the book with curiosity.

'Wonder what it can be, Dusty.'

'Something mighty interesting, if VENOM are after it.'

'You bet.'

'Let's hope the computer can help us.'

'We'll put it under the optical scanner.'

Matt placed the book on the surface in front of him and pressed a button. The optical scanner was switched on and its results came up immediately on the large screen that covered one wall. A computer printout of the book appeared with analytical tables, measurements and factual data displayed in its squares.

The computer voice was flat, impersonal and female.

'Historical data base reveals this book is evidence of the legend of the Mong Paco empire.'

'The *what*?' gulped Dusty.

'Legend claims the city of Mong Paco mysteriously vanished off the face of the earth some fifteen hundred years ago.'

The computer clicked and a new image was created on its screen. Looking rather like Pompeii, the noble city of Mong Paco was imposing and dignified. In the foreground was a computer graphic rendition of a superb idol that was covered in sparkling objects. It dominated the screen and made the two MASK agents whistle in awe.

The computer voice provided a commentary.

'They supposedly possessed a jewel-encrusted idol that was over three storeys tall. It is said that the idol protected the city with a cunning array of booby-traps!'

Dusty was thrilled. 'A jewel-encrusted idol. Yowee!'

'Today,' continued the computer, 'the estimated value of the idol would run into billions.'

'*That's* what VENOM is after,' realised Matt.

'I don't blame them,' said Dusty. 'Billions of dollars.'

'They must never get hold of that idol.'

'Sounds like a job for a full team, Matt.'

'I'll assemble them immediately.'

Matt pressed another button and a video camera swivelled around to focus on his face. He gave the command in a firm voice.

'Give me the data on the best agents for this mission.'

The screen flashed with static and then the face of Hondo MacLean came up alongside a computer graphic rendition of his MASK vehicle, Firecracker.

The computer voice supplied the pertinent details.

'Hondo MacLean – weapons specialist, tactical strategist. Vehicle Code Name – Firecracker. Co-pilot.'

'Approved,' said Matt.

Other faces appeared in turn on the screen as the voice described them. The next in line was Alex Sector whose full beard was a vivid contrast to his gleaming bald head.

'Alex Sector – computer and communications expert, research scientist. Transport – Rhino.'

'Approved.'

'Bruce Sato – mechanical engineer and design specialist. Vehicle Code Name – Rhino.'

'Approved.'

'Brad Turner – motorcycle and helicopter pilot. Vehicle Code Name – Condor.'

'Approved.'

'Buddie Hawkes – master of disguise, Intelligence expert. Vehicle Code Name – Firecracker. Co-pilot.'

'Approved.'

'What about me?' asked Dusty.

The computer responded in the same flat, unemotional voice.

'Dusty Hayes – auto and marine stunt driver. Vehicle Code Name – Gator.'

'Personnel approved,' announced Matt. 'Assemble Mobile Armoured Strike Kommand.'

As he gave the familiar order, he looked down at his watch and pressed a tiny button on it. The word MASK flashed up on a liquid-crystal display.

The wrist-watch sent its signal to the agents who had been selected.

Hondo MacLean, a history teacher at a nearby High School, was about to sink his teeth into a club sandwich when the call came. He handed the sandwich to one of his students, got up from the table and went out of the cafeteria at speed. The meal could wait.

Alex Sector, owner of an exotic pet store, was involved in feeding as well. He was tipping some powder into a large tank that housed rare tropical fish. When his wrist-watch started to flash, he turned away at once, handed the box of fishfood to a bemused customer and left the store without a word.

Bruce Sato, a brilliant toy designer, was working on a giant yoyo in his workshop. He was just trying it out when he was summoned on MASK business. Putting his latest toy aside, he went out at a brisk pace, moving from the world of children to that of intrigue, danger and high adventure.

Brad Turner, vocalist and guitarist with a rock group, was playing at a live concert when his watch signalled to him. Abandoning his song in the middle of a line, he lifted his guitar off and put it aside before striding off the stage.

Buddie Hawkes, an attendant at the Boulder Hill gas station, was operating a hydraulic lift that was slowly raising a car from the ground. When he got his call, he took his hand off the lever and hurried out of the garage. The car continued to rise higher and higher to the dismay of its bewildered owner.

MASK assignments were paramount.

The agents had been trained to respond instantly.

They knew they had to deal with a crisis situation.

VENOM was in action again!

Scott Trakker came into the Bullet Shuttle room with T-Bob. To reach MASK headquarters, they had to drive along a narrow tunnel that led to the secret complex beneath the Boulder Hill gas station. Matt might be interested in the Book of Power but his adopted son had another priority. All that he could think about was the pizza.

'Ready to go?' asked T-Bob.

'You bet. I want my piece of that pizza.'

'I still say it's a mistake to disobey your father.'

'No, it isn't,' replied the boy. 'Go to motorscooter mode.'

The robot converted at once into a motorscooter and drove around the room in top gear. Scott tried to get on but failed to do so.

'What are you waiting for?' said T-Bob.

'Stop kidding around!'

'Jump on.'

'Then slow down, will you?'

T-Bob came to a halt and Scott climbed astride. The robot entered the tunnel and bowled along at a steady speed. Since the tunnel had been designed for the Bullet Shuttle, its walls were round and smooth. T-Bob was slipping all over the place.

'Yi!' he complained.

'You're doing just great, T-Bob.'

'That pizza will be cold by the time we get there.'

'As long as there's still some left for me.'

'I just hope your father doesn't discover us.'

'Not a chance.'

'Whenever we ignore his orders, we seem to end up in trouble.'

'Quit worrying and just keep going.'

As they surged on through the tunnel, Scott was sure that he could smell the nice, fresh pizza that awaited him up ahead. He licked his lips and could almost taste his slice.

All the MASK agents arrived in the computer room with the minimum of delay. They gathered around Matt Trakker who was still standing at the main console. The Book of Power was now positioned beneath another device that explored it with a long, metal nozzle. The results of the analytical scan were displayed up on the large screen. All eyes watched as something rather unusual appeared on the computer readout.

'What in tarnation is *that*?' asked Buddie Hawkes.

The female monotone gave him his answer straight away.

'Pepperoni with double cheese.'

Dusty shrugged. 'My secret recipe is out!'

The other agents joined in the good-humoured laughter.

'Also,' warned the computer, 'electronic components sealed in the binding. Circuit board is at B-100 configuration.'

The computer readout displayed a detailed X-ray of the electronic components in the binding, complete with flashing LED lights.

Hondo MacLean recognised it at once.

'Better take care of that!' he cautioned. 'Looks like one of VENOM's tracking devices!'

'It is,' agreed Matt. 'That means they know where the book is.'

'And they'll be back to collect it,' added Dusty.

There was immediate confirmation of this fact. A klaxon went off with ear-shattering force and the computer voice gave the alert in a loud voice.

'Code Red! Enemy approaching MASK headquarters.'

Three VENOM vehicles came up on the screen.

'They're just a couple of miles away,' noted Buddie Hawkes.

'I suggest that we destroy that tracking device at once,' argued Alex Sector, pointing to the Book of Power.

'Too late,' said Buddie. 'They're almost here.'

'Then we've got no choice,' concluded Matt, taking command. 'This is it, men. Prepare for defence mode.'

The MASK agents sprung into action at once. They rushed to their stations and manned their respective weapons. A full-scale assault by VENOM was a serious threat to their whole organisation. They simply had to repel it somehow.

Defensive systems were activated with utmost urgency. The Boulder Hill gas station was transformed into bunker mode and hidden behind massive armoured doors. The gas pumps converted into high-power guns that could fire freeze rays and which swivelled on their base to give a wide firing range. On the mountain that loomed above the gas station, a hill turret opened and laser guns protruded.

As an additional means of defence, the huge boulder at the top of the mountain stood ready to be propelled down on the enemy.

Matt Trakker operated a console in the war room.

'No time for mistakes!' he urged.

VENOM

VENOM was out to destroy MASK headquarters.
It could be a fight to the death.
Matt and his agents were ready.

FOUR

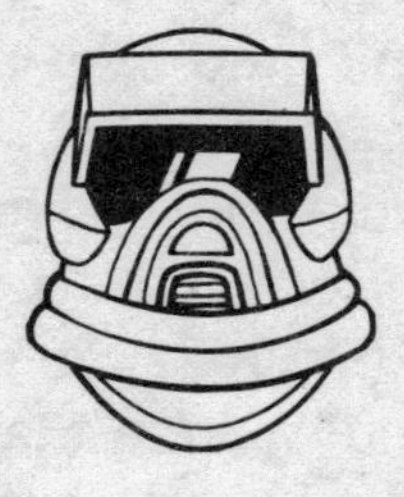

Miles Mayhem was leading the attack in Switchblade. Flanking him were Cliff Dagger in Jackhammer and Sly Rax on Piranha. All three men wore their masks. The VENOM vehicles screamed around a bend and saw the Boulder Hill gas station ahead of them.

Mayhem emitted a throaty cackle.

'Looks like we've been expected.'

Jackhammer immediately converted into an assault vehicle. Its front hood slid over the windshield for protection and its reciprocating cannons emerged through a grill. Its pop-up rear turret had rapid-fire guns that had a 360 degree swivel.

Piranha also went to attack mode. Protective steel

plating came up at the front and its recessed machine guns stood ready in the cowling. It could also discharge ground torpedoes. Forward-mounted machine-gun turrets turned the sidecar into a lethal arsenal.

Inside Switchblade, Mayhem listened to the bleeping sound of the homing beam. They were getting close to the Book of Power.

He snapped a command over the intercom.

'I want that book at all costs!'

Dagger responded at once. The rear turret of Jackhammer began to fire at the bunker. The air was suddenly alive with whizzing shells and crackling bullets. Some of them were on target.

Matt Trakker replied to the attack instantly.

'Deploy electronic force field!'

The gas pumps swivelled and fired electric bolts. They bounced against Jackhammer and surrounded it with a force field. The VENOM machine was now trapped in a kind of bubble. When it tried to escape, it kept banging itself against the invisible force field and rebounding.

Matt allowed himself a smile of amusement.

'He's bouncing like a rubber ball out there.'

Sly Rax now brought his weaponry into play.

'This oughta knock out that turret!' he growled.

His target was the hill turret high above them. He released a ground torpedo that angled upwards, hissing at speed. If it made contact, it would undoubtedly blast its target to pieces.

Hondo MacLean was manning the hill turret and he spotted the danger. His answer was immediate.

'Uh, uh – you don't mess with Hondo!'

Aiming his guns, he fired off a succession of lasers. They hit the torpedo and exploded it harmlessly in mid-air. One of the laser beams zizzed down to puncture the tyres on Piranha. The vehicle went into a wild spin.

'I'm going dizzy!' yelled Rax.

Hondo MacLean shook with laughter inside his turret.

'We've got a rubber ball and a spinning top!'

MASK was winning the battle so far.

But it was far from over.

Unaware of the contest being fought outside, Scott Trakker and T-Bob arrived at the computer room and peeped in. It was deserted. The boy's eyes went straight to the pizza box that stood by the main console. He chortled with glee and led the way across the room.

'I knew my nose would find it sooner or later.'

T-Bob converted back from motorscooter mode.

'I smell trouble,' said the robot.

'I smell pepperoni.'

Scott opened the pizza box and stepped back in surprise when he saw the Book of Power lying inside it.

'Hey!'

'It don't look like any pizza *I* ever saw,' noted T-Bob.

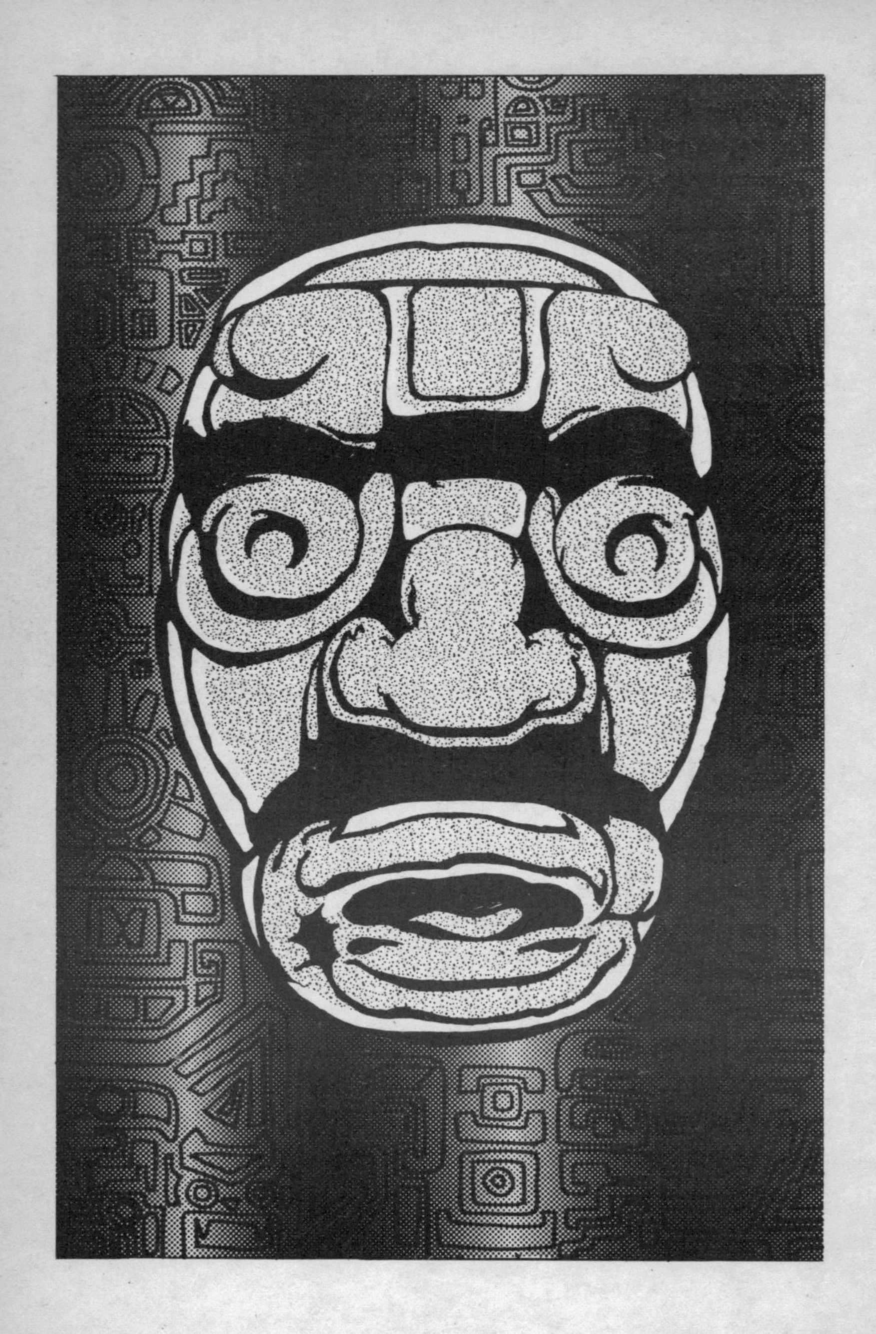

'What's this dumb old book doing here?'

'Dusty must have got his recipe wrong somehow.'

'I can't eat *this*!' complained the boy.

'Try reading it.'

'What?'

'Food for the mind.'

Scott picked up the book and flipped through the pages.

'Wow! Sure is weird writing.'

As he leafed through the book, a subliminal image appeared and flashed out at him two or three times. The image was that of the frightening face whose eyes now blazed with an uncanny light. Scott's face was aglow for a second and he blinked his eyes in wonderment.

He seemed to be in some kind of trance.

When he spoke, his voice was a dull monotone.

'What was that?'

'Yeah!' gulped T-Bob. 'What was *that*!'

'I have a mission,' intoned the boy.

'We're not chasing *another* pizza, are we?'

'I must obey the call.'

T-Bob went right up to him and studied him with curiosity.

'You look *weird*.'

'The mountain,' ordered Scott. 'Let's go.'

'You *sound* weird.'

'The mountain waits. We go.'

With the book under his arm, the boy walked away.

It was the conclusive piece of evidence for T-Bob.

'You *are* weird!'

Scott Trakker went past the Bullet Shuttle and stood by the entrance to the tunnel. He seemed to be in the grip of some alien force and his voice remained a strange monotone.

'Motorscooter mode!'

T-Bob changed at once and the boy mounted the saddle. They shot off down the tunnel but Scott was not really in control.

The Book of Power was telling him where to go.

Cliff Dagger was the first to notice the change. Having finally got out of the force field, he was firing on the bunker once more. As he glanced down at a screen on his dashboard, he saw the electronic signal starting to fade.

He flicked a switch to speak over the intercom.

'Hey! The tracking device is moving out of range.'

'We mustn't let that happen,' replied Mayhem.

'Our hands are full here,' said Dagger.

'Time to finish MASK off, then,' decided his leader.

Miles Mayhem had converted Switchblade to its helicopter mode and he was hovering over the bunker. Bullets, shells and lasers were flying everywhere but none of them were hitting their targets properly. It was the moment for more decisive action.

Mayhem pressed a button and Switchblade converted to jet mode in a flash. Its blades were retracted and two wings appeared. High-powered engines gave

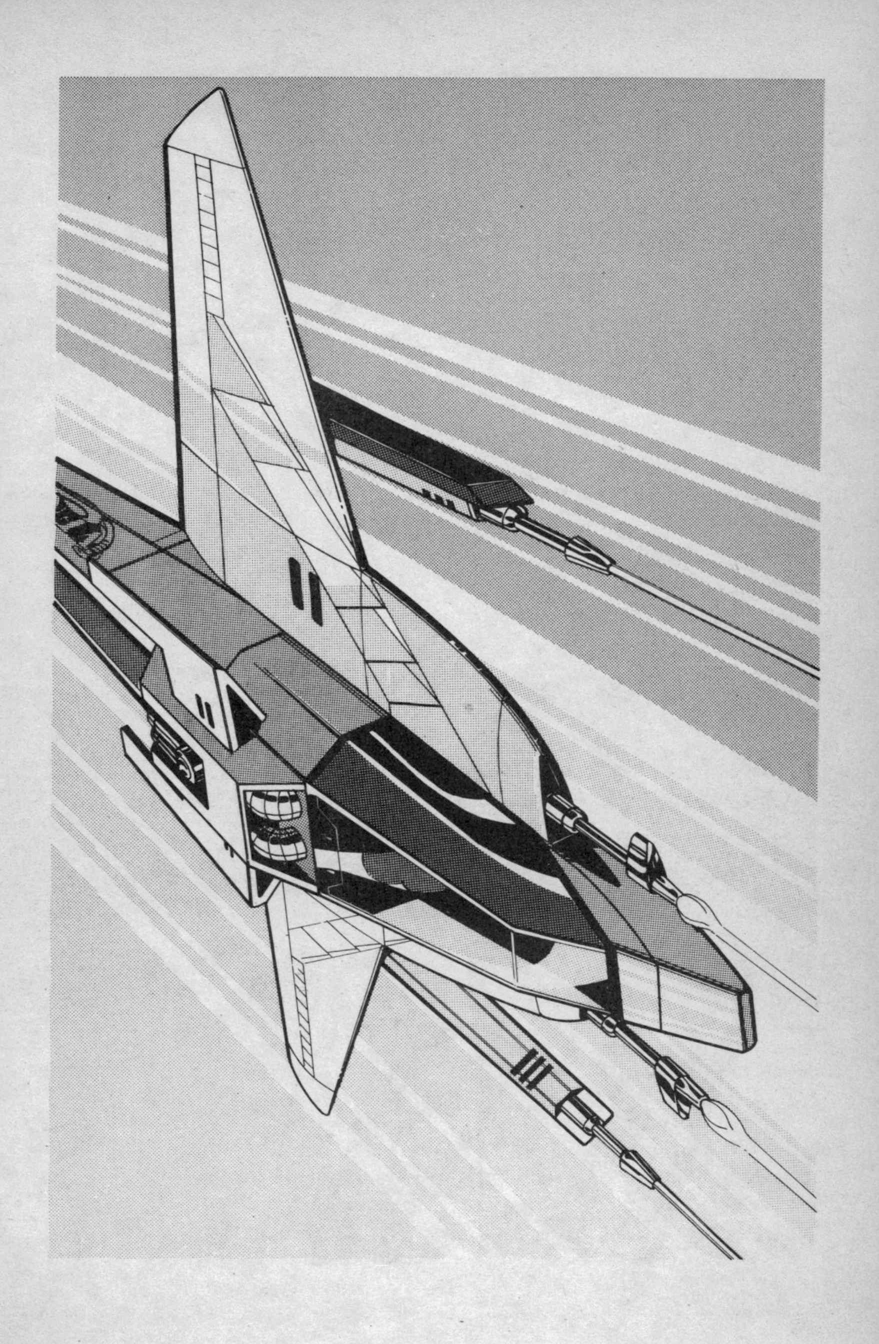

it extra thrust and it brought a deadly weapon into play. Rockets were fired from both wings. They zoomed towards the bunker with the aim of destroying it completely.

The VENOM commander gave an evil chuckle.

'This should wipe them out once and for all!'

Matt Trakker saw the danger on the monitors in the war room.

'We've got problems, Buddie,' he warned.

'Nothing we can't handle,' promised Buddie Hawkes.

He flicked a switch on the console in front of him.

'Have a taste of anti-gravity!' he said.

The anti-gravity cannon rose up in the gas station shop and fired directly at the approaching rockets. Surrounding them with an anti-gravity beam, they made the rockets loop around and head back the way that they had come.

The tables had now been turned on VENOM.

Mayhem saw the rockets flashing back towards him.

'Oh no!'

He jabbed at a button in desperation and Switchblade converted back to helicopter mode. The machine soared upwards in the nick of time. Hurtling beneath it, the rockets went on until they exploded with a reverberating bang against the side of the mountain.

Miles Mayhem was now bitter and vengeful.

'Smash them, Dagger!' he ordered over the intercom.

'Leave it to me,' replied his henchman.

'Hit 'em with everything you've got.'

Jackhammer deployed all its armoury and a huge volley of ammunition and laser bolts poured from it. Smoke and dust obscured the view for several minutes. When it cleared, the extent of the damage could be seen and it sent a wicked thrill of joy through the VENOM ranks.

The bunker was just a massive pile of debris.

MASK had been destroyed.

Miles Mayhem roared in triumph as Switchblade circled overhead.

'We blasted them to rubble!'

'It was easy,' boasted Dagger.

'Yeah,' grunted Sly Rax, who had now repaired his tyres. 'When we gave 'em the works, it did the trick.'

'That'll teach 'em!' added Dagger.

'Now we find the Book of Power!' declared Mayhem. 'Follow me.'

Switchblade flew away from the bunker with Jackhammer and Piranha in pursuit. Confident that they had obliterated their mortal enemy, VENOM was withdrawing from the scene of battle.

Their confidence was not well-founded.

As soon as they had vanished, a pattern of waves rolled over the supposedly ruined bunker. When the waves dissolved, the Boulder Hill gas station stood there quite unharmed.

Down in the war room, the MASK agents laughed.

Matt congratulated Brad Turner with a slap on the back.

'Great work, Brad. Your hologram sure fooled VENOM.'

'It never fails,' replied Brad.

His unique Hocus Pocus mask had saved them again. Under the cover of the smoke and dusk, he had projected a hologram image of a ruined bunker. Mayhem and his cohorts had made the mistake of believing what they thought they saw.

Bruce Sato contributed his own piece of wisdom.

'There is more than one way to pull the wool over the eyes of the fox.'

'But why did they *leave*?' wondered Alex Sector.

'Yes,' agreed Dusty. 'I thought they were after the book.'

'They were,' said Matt. 'That tracking device led them here.'

'So why didn't they try to grab the book?' asked Hondo.

'Doesn't make sense,' decided Buddie Hawkes.

'Unless the book is no longer here,' suggested Alex.

'Of course, it's here,' argued Dusty. 'Isn't it?'

'Let's find out,' ordered Matt.

He led the way back to the computer room.

But the Book of Power was a long way away now. It had been carried to a distant region that had an ugly, misshapen mountain. With the book under his arm, Scott Trakker walked on in a trance. T-Bob crept along

behind him, casting nervous glances up at the menacing rock above him. The mountain had the same unnerving quality as the frightening face.

For a brief moment, Scott's voice returned to normal.

'Somehow, I felt I must come here.'

'Why?' asked the robot.

'I don't know.'

'I do,' said T-Bob. 'This mountain's as weird as you are!'

The boy looked up at the bare rock. A small portion of it now looked exactly like the frightening face on the front of the Book of Power. Scott went into a full trance again and his voice was hollow.

'We go on.'

'Let's go back,' begged the robot.

'This way.'

'No – *thataway*!'

They walked towards a cavernous opening in the mountain.

'Here it is,' announced Scott.

'Look at that mouth!' warned T-Bob, shrinking back.

'It isn't a mouth,' explained his companion. 'It's the doorway to Mong Paco. We go inside.'

T-Bob's metallic teeth were now chattering noisily.

'We!' he exclaimed. 'Mong Paco!'

'Follow.'

They went in through the entrance and found themselves in a dank, eerie cave with strange, glistening walls. T-Bob was now shaking with terror but Scott seemed quite unafraid.

'Somehow, I just had to come to this place,' he said.

He tightened his grip on the book under his arm and the tracking device fell out of the binding and landed on the ground. Neither he nor T-Bob noticed it.

The robot's attention was fixed on something else. A huge, mysterious shadow had fallen aross them. T-Bob whirled around in a panic and saw something that made his eyes widen.

'Scott – look out!'

FIVE

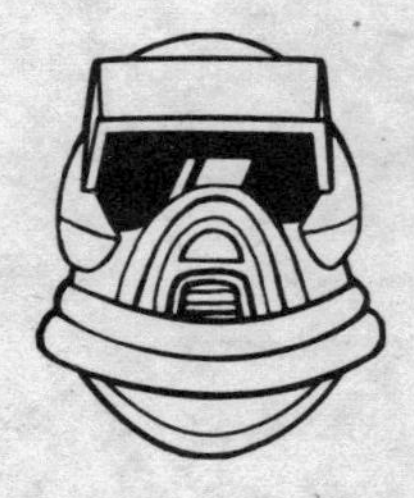

Matt Trakker and the MASK agents were completely baffled. When they got back to the computer room, there was no sign of the Book of Power.

Matt gazed down at the empty pizza box.

'I can't understand it. Who could have taken the book?'

'There's no way VENOM could have gotten in here,' said Buddie.

'It's just vanished into thin air,' observed Hondo.

Dusty nodded. 'Like one of my pizzas.'

Alex Sector worked the controls beside the video screen.

'The video alarm was activated by someone,' he

explained. 'I'll play back the tape and identify the thief.'

'This should be very interesting,' added Matt.

He stood in front of the screen with his men and watched carefully as the video showed Scott and T-Bob entering the room. When the boy opened the pizza box and took out the book, Matt realised what had brought his son to the room. Evidently, he had been after a slice of what he thought was one of Dusty's special pizzas.

Up on the screen, Scott flicked through the pages of the Book of Power and was hit by the subliminal message that flashed across his face. His manner altered at once.

'What's happened to him?' asked Buddie.

'He looks like a zombie,' commented Brad.

'No,' replied Hondo. 'He's in some kind of trance.'

'That book put the influence on him,' agreed Bruce.

The video showed Scott and T-Bob leaving the computer room.

'Where are they going now?' wondered Dusty.

'Wherever that book is leading them,' said Hondo.

Matt Trakker saw the peril that lay ahead.

'If VENOM's following that homing device, Scott will be walking straight into a trap!'

'We've got to save him somehow,' urged Brad.

'And T-Bob,' reminded Dusty.

'Don't forget that book,' said Bruce, sagely. 'In the hands of the enemy, it will be used against us.'

'You're right there,' agreed Matt.

He turned to Alex who was checking a scope. It began to emit a faint bleeping sound. Alex sighed.

'What's the situation?' asked Matt.

'The computer's locked into the signal but the transmission point is too far away.'

'We need another means of tracking them,' said Buddie.

Matt Trakker looked around his men and smiled.

'The Spectrum mask will take care of that. Let's move it!'

They ran from the room with great urgency.

A rapidly-moving escalator took them up to a thick metal door. On a verbal command from Matt, the door swung open to reveal a semi-circular room with a collection of masks hanging from the smooth walls. Electronic equipment was fixed into the ceiling high above. There was a subdued energy about the whole place.

On the floor were pre-marked spaces, arranged in a circle. As the men entered the room, they took up their designated positions and formed a circle that looked inwards.

The door of the energiser room closed behind them.

Matt Trakker took up his own position and completed the circle. The mask-charging ritual was vitally important and he looked around to check that all his agents were completely ready.

'Stand by for mask charging!'

There was a constant electronic whine throughout the process. From above and behind each man, long

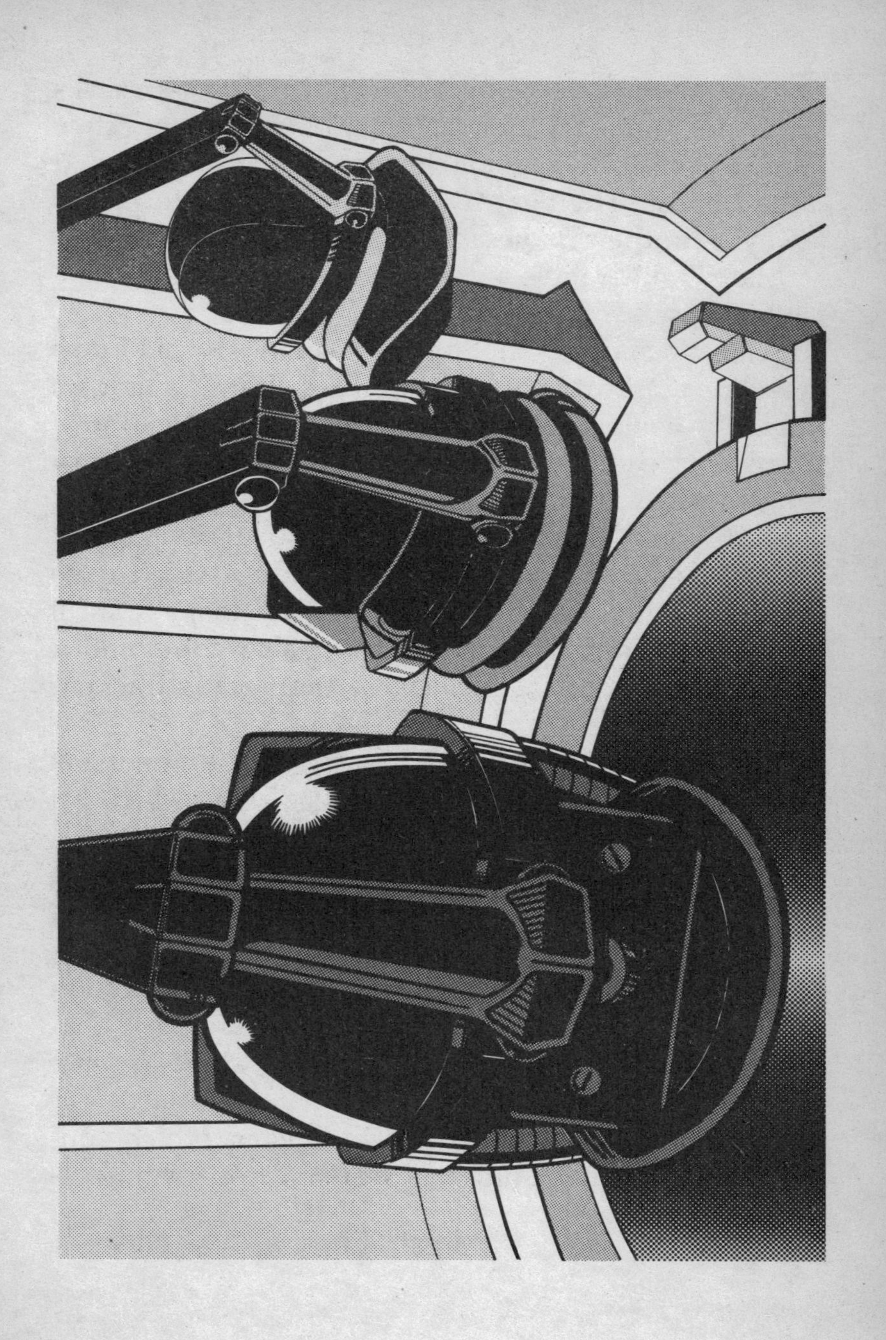

armature arms descended to lift the various masks from the walls. The metal arms held the respective masks over each man so that they could reach up and touch them. The agents carefully angled the masks away from their bodies.

Matt Trakker gave a curt order.

'Energise!'

A laser beam was shot from the ceiling. It split into a dazzling starburst pattern that threw frantic shadows on to the walls. Each ray of the laser penetrated one of the masks to energise it. The men were suffused with a bright, warm, uplifting glow.

Each one of them had his own particular mask.

Matt Trakker stood below Spectrum, which gave him free-fall abilities and which could make a shrill noise to disturb a foe. Spectrum also contained a mini-oscilloscope that acted as a high-grade tracking system.

Brad Turner waited under Hocus Pocus, the mask that could project holographic images to bamboozle an enemy.

Bruce Sato's choice was Lifter, so called because it could fire an anti-gravity beam that enabled him to lift and move heavy objects.

Alex Sector, the oldest man in the team, would soon be wearing Jackrabbit, a high-powered mask that allowed him rocket flight and thus the ability to take off like a jackrabbit.

Hondo MacLean was beneath Blaster, which contained an Internal Guidance System for his shoulder-launched lasers and made him a particularly formidable warrior.

The mask belonging to Dusty Hayes was named Backlash because it could fire shock waves on land or underwater.

Buddie Hawkes, the master of disguise, was holding Penetrator, which enabled both its user and his vehicle to move through solid objects like a ghost walking through a wall.

Seven dedicated men with seven special masks.

And a mission to defeat VENOM.

A fierce electronic buzz was heard then the entire floor began to rise. The agents were able to take the masks from the arms that held them and put them on.

Matt Trakker pulled on Spectrum and gave the command.

'To the transports!'

The garage at the rear of the Boulder Hill gas station was filled with vehicles awaiting repair or servicing. The rear wall of the garage suddenly opened up and the cars disappeared as electromagnetic arms reached out to pull them off to unseen racks.

From the floor, rising dramatically on hydraulic lifts, the MASK vehicles came into view. A second later, the agents themselves arrived on their elevated platform. With their masks in place, they ran to their respective machines.

When the garage door opened, they zoomed out.

Matt Trakker was at the controls of Thunder Hawk.

The sports car converted to jet mode at once and he soared into the sky. Far below him, his colleagues kept their machines in regular mode and drove along the road at top speed.

Matt issued another order.

'Spectrum mask – scan!'

The mini-oscilloscope was activated and it began to produce a regular bleep. Matt listened until the sound became louder.

'I've got him!' he announced over the intercom.

'We're right behind you, Matt,' replied Bruce.

'Seems to be coming from that mountain.'

Matt brought Thunder Hawk in to land and converted back to sports car mode. He was now at the head of the other MASK vehicles. Towering above him not far ahead, was the weird, misshapen mountain with the frightening face on its side.

The MASK agents thundered on to attempt their rescue bid.

Miles Mayhem was also listening to the sound from his tracking system. Switchblade was still in helicopter mode. Jackhammer and Piranha were tailing him on the ground.

He contacted both henchmen over his intercom.

'The signal's getting much stronger.'

'That means we're close,' said Rax.

'The Book of Power will soon be mine,' added Mayhem.

'But who moved it in the first place?' asked Dagger.

'What?' snarled his leader.

'Who took it from Boulder Hill?'

'Good point,' agreed Rax. 'Someone made a run with it. One of those MASK agents must still be alive.'

'Impossible!' decided Mayhem. 'We killed them all.'

'Then who stole the book?' persisted Dagger.

'That's what we'll find out.'

Mayhem flicked a switch and the bleeping sound was amplified. He saw the strange mountain looming up and smiled. They were almost there.

The lost idol of Mong Paco would soon be his.

The MASK vehicles arrived at the mountain before VENOM. Matt noticed that Spectrum was now emitting a loud, almost continuous noise.

'The signal is coming from *inside* the mountain.'

His voice could be heard by all the agents in their respective vehicles. Alex Sector was in Rhino, the heavy truck that was being driven by Bruce Sato. Sitting at his computer station, Alex fiddled with the controls and watched some wavy lines appear on a dial.

'It checks out,' he said. 'The sonar scanner indicates that the mountain is apparently quite hollow.'

Hondo MacLean responded from Firecracker.

'Then Scott's just *gotta* be inside!'

Buddie Hawkes, his co-pilot, peered through the windscreen.

'I don't see any openings, though.'

'That doesn't matter,' promised Brad Turner in Condor. 'All we need is a blast of anti-matter.'

Brad hit a button and Condor shot an anti-matter ray straight at the mountain. It struck the rock and melted a large, tunnel-sized hole in it. They now had their own private entrance.

Matt sent his congratulations into the microphone.

'Good work, Brad,' he said. 'Okay, men – roll in! Let's just hope that nobody else finds Scott first!'

The MASK agents went in through the still sizzling opening. What none of them realised was that they were under surveillance. Watching their every move was a monk, dressed in robes identical to those worn by the other monks. Beneath his hood, his face was impassive.

Thunder Hawk blazed the trail through the cavernous interior of the mountain then Matt spotted something which made him slow the vehicle to a halt. The other MASK machines pulled up as well and parked beside him. Led by Matt, the agents got out and walked forward.

The sight which greeted them was truly breathtaking.

Marble pillars were scattered on the ground. The debris of a once magnificent temple stood near a large arena that had fallen into decay. Public buildings, houses, statues and ornaments could be seen everywhere but they were all in a dilapidated condition.

The mountain was not merely hollow. It contained

MASK

the ruins of what had obviously once been a proud and beautiful city. Even in its sad state, it still possessed a wistful dignity.

Dusty Hayes recalled the picture he had seen on the screen back in the computer room. He knew exactly where they were.

'The Lost City of Mong Paco. Oooooh weeee!'

They stared at it with a mixture of awe and fascination.

SIX

The main chamber of the cavern had several levels. While his colleagues were still absorbing the glorious view, Alex Sector turned to Matt Trakker.

'Have you gotten a reading on Scott yet?'

Matt adjusted the controls on his Spectrum mask. The wave pattern and the bleeps were now much more erratic. He frowned.

'Scott's signal is irregular inside here. There's too much interference from the rock formations.'

'Don't worry,' said Bruce, putting a consoling hand on his arm. 'We'll find him, Matt.'

The MASK agents set off in single file. When they reached another, smaller chamber, Alex reminded them of something important.

'Be careful,' he warned. 'Remember what the legend said about booby-traps. They're all around us.'

Dusty confirmed the fact by pointing ahead.

'Hey!' he called. 'Speaking of booby-traps . . .'

He indicated the cross hairs of a cunning device that would activate a huge boulder balanced precariously on the tip of a ledge.

'Leave this to me,' boasted Dusty. 'I'm the path-finder.'

They followed him with great care as he walked around the booby trap but they were not out of danger yet. Dusty's foot accidentally dislodged a small rock which set off another booby-trap.

Stone doors suddenly dropped down from above to seal them into the chamber and sand began to pour in at speed through numerous openings. The men reacted in horror. They could be buried alive.

'Sand!' noted Hondo. 'I'll take care of it!'

He adjusted his position then gave the command.

'Hot shot – fire!'

His mask obeyed the order and shoulder-launched lasers shot towards the sand. Unfortunately, they were ineffective. The sand was gushing in so quickly that it broke up the beams, absorbed the blast and kept on coming. All that Hondo's lasers had done was to melt some blobs of sand together.

Within seconds, the men were up to their waist in sand.

It was a terrifying moment but they were equal to it.

Dusty Hayes leapt into action.

'Firing Backlash mask!'

Violent shock waves broke through the sand and caused one of the stone doors to crack open. Matt and his agents crawled through to safety at once. They had defied the first booby-trap.

Dusty looked back at the chamber, now filled with sand.

'That was closer than a near-sighted gopher to a turnip patch.'

Brad Turner had the feeling there was worse to come.

'I get the feeling we haven't seen *anything* yet.'

They were in a corridor and it ended in a solid wall. Set into the rock face were three mysterious-looking doors. Each had a large iron ring as its handle.

Matt Trakker wanted to cover every option.

'I say we split up and give them all a try.'

'Good idea,' agreed Alex.

'Who's coming with me?' asked Buddie.

The men chatted amiably as they broke up into groups. They entered the three doors at the same time. None of them realised that they were being observed from a ledge by another monk. From the moment they had entered the cavern, they had been watched.

Having gone through three separate doors, the agents were surprised and disappointed when they all emerged into the same room. It seemed innocent enough at first. There were ornate carvings on the walls and on the columns that held up the ceiling. The room was very much in the style of the city of Mong Paco.

Alex Sector sensed the danger immediately.

'Careful, mates,' he cautioned. 'Something's funny here.'

He was right.

The three doors slammed shut of their own accord and a loud grinding noise was heard as two of the walls began to close in on them.

They were caught in another trap.

Dusty looked around. 'I get a feeling this place is gonna be too close for comfort.'

'I knew it!' said Brad. 'I knew it'd be something like this.'

'Try the doors!' ordered Matt.

They did so but all three were locked.

The agents threw themselves against the moving walls in a futile attempt to hold them back. Grinding relentlessly on, the heavy stone was going to crush them to powder unless they took evasive action.

'It's no use!' yelled Hondo.

Brad heaved against a wall with all his strength but it slowly forced him backwards. Without warning, razor-sharp spikes popped out from behind the ornate carvings on both walls. They just missed Brad's outstretched arms.

'I'm beginning to get the point,' he said.

The two walls were now within a few feet of each other. Within a couple of minutes, the agents would be squeezed to death. It was time for emergency measures.

Dusty aimed his mask at the base of a pillar.

'Backlash – fire!'

The powerful beam shot out from his mask and hit the pillar with a sonic boom. It cracked at once and fell so that it was jammed on a diagonal between the two moving walls. It slowed them down but did not stop the movement altogether. The agents were glad of their brief respite.

'Now to get out of this squeeze play,' said Buddie.

'And fast!' urged Brad, seeing the pillar start to crack under the strain. 'Do your stuff, Hondo.'

Hondo aimed his mask at a stationary wall.

'Fire!' he commanded.

Several well-placed lasers zapped the stone and burned a large hole in it. The MASK agents now had a means of escaping their doom.

'Move it!' ordered Matt. 'The pillar's crumbling.'

The men dived through the hole as fast as they could. Bruce was the last to try to leave and he encountered trouble. Tripping and falling, he somehow caught his boot on one of the spikes. The pillar was now breaking up into pieces and the walls moved remorselessly closer.

Bruce felt that he would be squeezed to a pulp.

Matt Trakker came back to the hole in the wall.

'Bruce!' he exclaimed. 'Don't worry. I'll help you.'

'It's no use, Matt. Get out.'

But the MASK leader was not going to abandon one

of his men to such a horrible death. Leaping back into the room, he pulled the boot from the spike, got a grip under Bruce's arms and yanked him out through the hole just in time.

The moving walls met behind them with an awesome thud.

Miles Mayhem had now reached the mountain and was hovering over it in his helicopter. Jackhammer and Piranha waited below. The VENOM commander looked in vain for an opening in the strange, distorted rock.

'The book's tracking signal is strongest here,' he announced. 'There must be a cavern inside. Rax!'

'Yeah?' replied his henchman.

'Blast a hole in that mountain.'

Sly Rax pressed a button and Piranha converted to attack mode. He launched two ground torpedoes that streaked towards their target.

'This oughta do the job,' he grunted.

Slamming into the mountain, the torpedoes created a huge hole. Mayhem brought Switchblade down so that it could fly straight in through the smoking entrance.

'Come on!' he snarled.

Followed by Jackhammer and Piranha, the helicopter made its way through the hollow interior until it reached the ruins of an old temple. Switchblade came into land, then its engine stopped. The other VENOM vehicles came to a halt beside it.

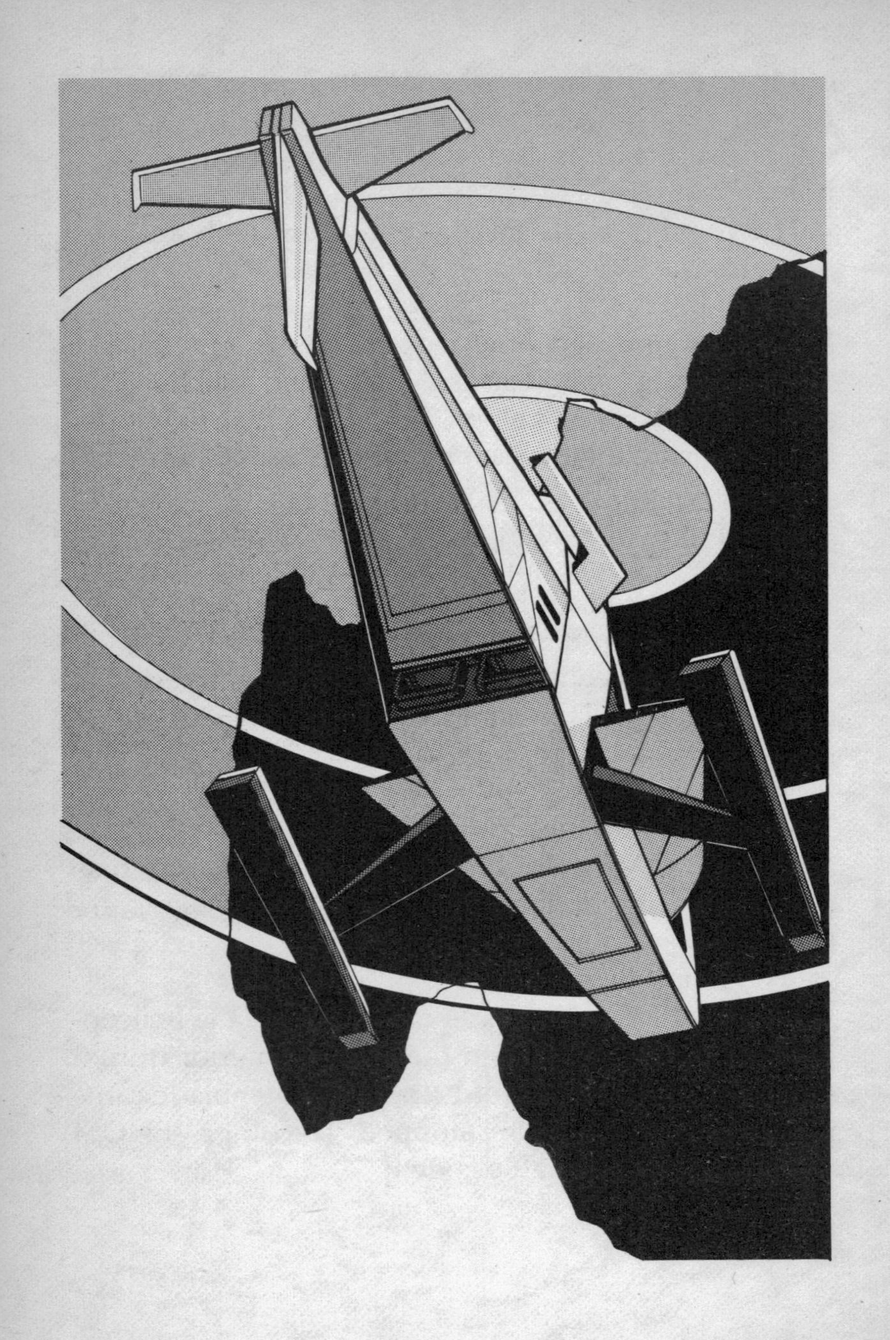

'Now what, Mayhem?' asked Dagger.

'I'm going to deal *personally* with whoever stole my book!'

MASK agents came running out from behind some rock formations and startled them. Matt Trakker had overheard Mayhem's threat.

'Sorry, Mayhem,' he replied. 'You're going to deal personally with *me*!'

'I thought we finished these guys off,' said Rax.

'We've come back to haunt you!' retorted Matt.

Dagger leapt from his vehicle and gave an order.

'Torch – on!'

His Torch mask responded and flames zipped towards Alex Sector.

The MASK agent activated his own mask.

'Jackrabbit – fly!'

Alex leapt high into the air and the flames passed beneath him.

Dusty Hayes now brought his mask into play.

'This'll shake 'em up,' he said. 'Backlash – fire!'

Shockwaves were launched straight at the VENOM leader. He was knocked back hard and went somersaulting through the air. As soon as he hit the ground again, Mayhem picked himself up and bolted towards the nearest exit.

Matt Trakker led the pursuit.

'After him!'

But the chase was short-lived.

In hitting Mayhem with the shockwaves, Dusty had in fact knocked him over a booby-trap to safety. As the

MASK agents went rushing after their enemy, they now became victims of the trap.

There was a rumbling sound and the floor opened up beneath them like a trap door. They fell through it at once. Their cries echoed.

'He-e-e-e-lp!'

'Yiiiii!'

'Ohhhhhhh!'

'Whoah!!!!'

The men fell through the air then landed on a tunnel-like slide that was made out of smooth stone. The slide was sharply angled so they were not hurt by the fall but they now found themselves plummeting downwards and speeding around treacherous curves as if trapped on some kind of mad roller-coaster.

The slide barely cleared some low ridges in the cavern and they had to be careful not to hit some of the overhanging rock. Brad Turner was the last of the swiftly tumbling line. He looked around desperately for a source of help.

He saw a long, jagged stalactite hanging from the ceiling.

'If only I can grab that thing!'

As he slid further down, he made a tremendous effort and caught hold of it. Brad now clung to it for dear life.

'Whew!' he said. 'I did it!'

There was an ominous crack. When he gazed up, he saw that the stalactite was breaking off under his weight. He dropped back down to the slide with the great jagged stalactite right behind him.

'Whoa!' he shouted. 'It's after me!'

The other MASK agents looked back up the slide. They saw the massive projectile hurtling down the slope towards them. It was big enough and sharp enough to cut them all to shreds.

Hondo MacLean gave the warning.

'Look out – it's after *us*!'

They were now in a worse predicament than ever.

SEVEN

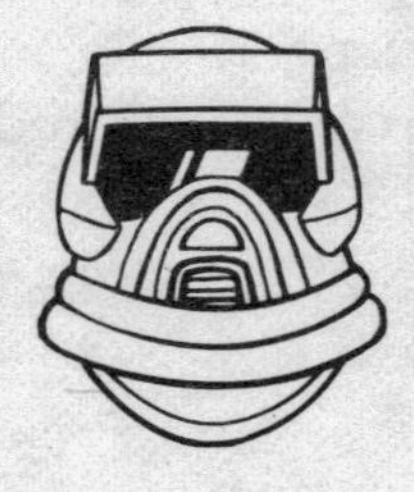

Matt Trakker and his agents tumbled helplessly down the steep incline. The stalactite pursued them with a vengeance and got closer and closer. Some of them braced themselves to feel its terrifying impact but their leader tried to avert the danger. As he came around a curve in the slide, he looked back and aimed his mask at the projectile.

'Spectrum mask – on!'

The laser beam hit the stalactite with such force that it melted into steam. Certain death had been avoided once more.

An opening soon appeared in the side of the tunnel.

'Hang on!' warned Brad.

The MASK agents tumbled out through the opening

and fell through the air again before making a soft landing on loose earth. They were on a lower level of the main cavern only a short distance from their vehicles. They got up at once and dusted themselves off.

'To the transports!' ordered Matt.

Mayhem and his henchmen were not far away. When they saw their enemies running towards the parked vehicles, they knew they were in for another tense battle.

'They're back,' said Mayhem. 'Keep them busy while I go after that book!'

'Leave it to us,' replied Dagger.

'Yeah,' boasted Rax. 'We'll zap 'em good!'

The MASK agents had now leapt into their respective machines.

'We've got to find Scott before VENOM does,' announced Matt. 'Defence mode!'

Hondo MacLean's pickup truck converted at once.

'My hypno-headlights oughta take care of them for a while,' he said. 'Take a look at this, guys!'

He threw a switch and his hypno-headlights concentrated their mesmeric beam on Jackhammer. As the rays hit Dagger's face, his eyes glazed over and he froze. With nobody controlling it, his machine careered into some rubble and was brought to a sudden halt.

Sly Rax was aiming his attack at Rhino, firing his machine guns with sinister relish. The bullets were

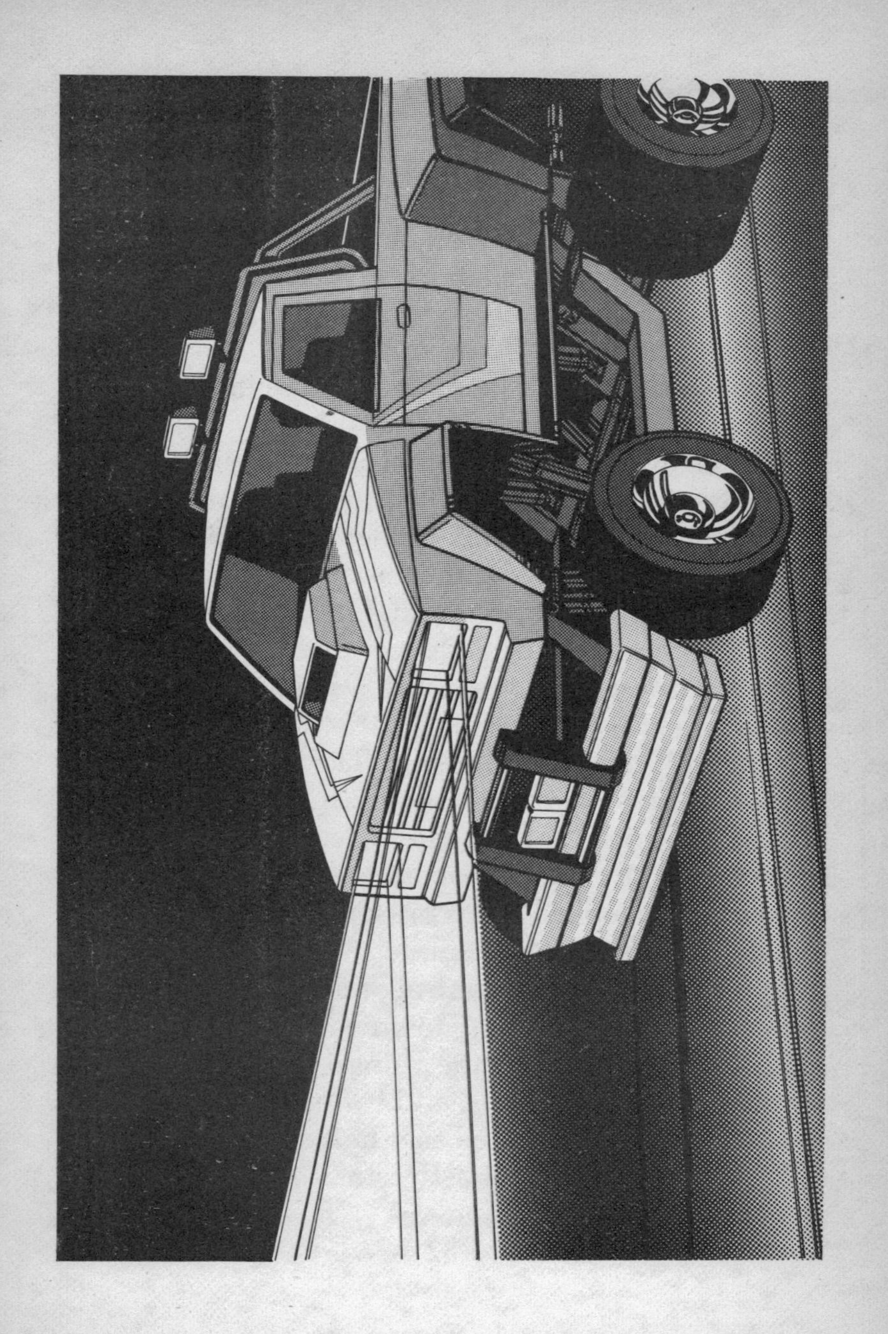

strafing the ground in front of the MASK vehicle. Bruce Sato decided to teach Rax a lesson.

'Time to make the fox run from the scarecrow!'

He adjusted some controls on his dashboard and the Rhino smokestacks converted to laser cannons that fired several prolonged bursts. Rax saw the beams coming at him and swerved to avoid them, causing the Piranha to crash into some rubble.

Two enemy vehicles were now immobilised.

Matt Trakker was now in Thunder Hawk which had converted to jet mode so that it could fire its wing cannons at Switchblade. The attack was making the helicopter go higher and higher inside the cavern. Mayhem searched for a means of escape and saw a narrow entrance above him that led to another chamber. He guided Switchblade towards the exit.

Brad Turner saw what the VENOM leader was doing.

'Oh, no, you don't!' he said. 'Hocus Pocus – fire!'

Several rays beamed instantly from the mask and soared to the roof of the cavern. As Mayhem approached the narrow opening, the hologram rays created what looked like a brick wall directly ahead.

'Oh, no!' yelled Mayhem.

In his panic, he lost control of Switchblade and the helicopter came spinning downwards until it skidded along the ground into the ruins. All three VENOM vehicles were now dazed and battered.

Miles Mayhem decided that he had had enough.

It was time to beat a hasty retreat.

'Let's get out of here!' he shouted.

'What about the Book of Power?' asked Dagger.

'Yeah,' grunted Rax. 'You gonna leave that here?'

'My life is more important than any book!' roared Mayhem.

Dagger and Rax looked at the agents who surrounded them.

They quickly agreed with their leader.

Switchblade, Jackhammer and Piranha limped out of the cavern as fast as they could. VENOM had been put to flight again. The MASK agents gave a cheer.

'You haven't seen the last of me, MASK!' threatened Mayhem. 'I'll be back! Just wait!'

Matt Trakker got out of Thunder Hawk and beckoned his men over to him. The most urgent task had still not been completed.

'We must locate Scott somehow,' he said.

'Let's hope he missed those booby-traps!' observed Dusty.

'There's enough of them around!' sighed Brad.

'We'll split up and search,' declared Matt.

Bruce Sato waved them into silence with his hand.

'Thought I heard something,' he explained.

They listened intently but no sound came.

Bruce shrugged. 'I must have been mistaken.'

But he was not. A distant voice echoed in another chamber.

'Dad! Dad!'

'It's Scott!' yelled Matt in delight.

'We're here! We're here!' piped another voice.

'That's T-Bob,' identified Dusty.

Boy and robot came sprinting into the chamber and stopped to wave to the agents. Scott was out of breath but he seemed unharmed. He was no longer in a trance and his voice was back to normal.

'Hi!' he called.

'Are you okay?' said Matt.

'Fine.'

'Terrific,' added T-Bob.

'Where've you been?' asked Matt.

'Everywhere, Dad.'

'It's been great fun,' noted the robot, cheerfully.

'Thank goodness we found you, Scott.'

Matt Trakker's joy turned to fear at once. A shadow fell across the boy and then a mysterious figure in robes and a hood approached from behind. Scott appeared to be in grave danger.

'Look out!' warned Matt.

'Why, Dad?'

'Behind you!'

The boy turned around and saw the monk there. Raising his staff in the air, the monk looked as if he was about to strike Scott and the MASK agents shouted a protest. It was not needed. The monk put his arm around the boy's shoulders.

Matt Trakker saw that the man had something under his other arm.

It was the Book of Power.

'Who is that guy?' he asked.

'Oh, he's my new friend,' explained Scott, airily.

'Yeah,' said T-Bob. 'He's a monkey.'

'Not a monkey!' corrected the boy. 'A *monk*!'

'What's the difference?' asked the robot.

'Just you try feeding *him* on peanuts!' suggested Dusty.

'Welcome to you all,' said the monk.

'Who are you?' asked Matt.

'Follow me, Mr Trakker, and all will become clear.'

The monk led the way into a large ceremonial chamber. It was an imposing structure with elaborate carvings all around and a real sense of history to it. Matt and his colleagues glanced around with candid interest. It was very different from the high technology world in which they operated.

Still holding the Book of Power, the monk told his tale.

'Let me explain,' he began. 'For many centuries, the descendants of Mong Paco have been searching for their lost city. We could never find it. The Book of Power was said to be the key to the mystery but we could not decipher it.'

'So how did you get here?' wondered Matt.

'That was my doing, Dad!' said Scott, proudly.

'You?'

'Yes. When I flipped through the pages of that book, it put me into a sort of trance.'

'We saw that on the video playback,' recalled Alex.

'I was led straight here,' added the boy.

'So was I,' piped T-Bob.

'We followed young Scott,' said the monk. 'He

brought us to the end of our quest. We are forever grateful.'

'*We*?' repeated Matt.

'You mean there's more than one of you?' asked Dusty.

'Oh, yes, my friend. We are more than one.'

He motioned with his staff. It bore the frightening face.

Dozens of monks appeared from all over the place. They were dressed alike but they did not carry a staff. The men had concealed themselves behind the rocks to watch the final battle between MASK and VENOM. Only now did they feel safe enough to come out of hiding.

'Ohhh weeee!' yelled Dusty. 'I don't believe it!'

'I've never seen so many monkeys,' said T-Bob.

'*Monks*!' reminded Scott, nudging him.

'Sorry,' apologised the robot.

The monk who had explained about the lost city now rested his staff against the wall of the chamber. He told the agents why he and his colleagues had remained out of sight.

'At first, we thought you were evil like that Mayhem.'

'Nobody is evil like *him*,' sighed Matt Trakker.

'When we saw you drive them away,' continued the monk. 'we knew that you were good. The same as us.'

'Not *quite* the same as you,' observed Bruce.

'We try to lead a holy life,' said the man.

'Our task is to fight against evil,' added Matt. 'We

don't claim to be holy but we hope we make a holy life possible for others.'

'Only one thing I don't understand,' admitted Dusty.

'What's that, my friend?' asked the monk.

'How in tarnation did you cause that rockslide earlier on?'

'Quite easily,' explained the monk. 'There was no magic involved. I simply loosened that big boulder with my staff.' He looked around and was baffled. 'Where is it? My staff was right here!'

'*There* it is,' said Matt Trakker, pointing a finger.

T-Bob was playing with it. He was twirling the staff as if it were a baton. Scott yelled a warning to him.

'Put that down!'

'I'm just playing,' said the robot. 'Maybe I'd be a better baton twirler than a football player.'

T-Bob set the staff down against a shallow indentation in the rock. The results were quite dramatic. The staff glowed like a strip of fluorescent light and the entire wall started to shake.

Scott and the others stepped back in concern as the wall began to split open like huge double doors. Something came into view which made them all gape. It was three storeys high and covered from top to bottom in precious jewels.

'Wow!' exclaimed Scott. 'I don't believe it!'

'It's the legendary idol of Mong Paco!' said Alex.

The monks were thrown into a frenzy of excitement.

'The legend comes true! You are to rule!'

They mobbed the frightened T-Bob and bowed in front of him. The robot had no idea what was going on and tried to back away. The leading monk once more provided the explanation.

'The legend says that the one who finds the statue shall become our leader.'

T-Bob was aghast. '*Me*!'

The monk looked at him then gave an understanding smile.

'Maybe in this case – *not*!'

'Whew!' gasped the robot in relief.

Matt Trakker led the laughter.

Another MASK assignment had come to a happy end.

If you have enjoyed Book Of Power, you might like to read some other MASK titles from Knight Books

Get ready for

MASK 5 – PANDA POWER

When all the Chinese pandas are stolen from the nature preserves, MASK is not long in finding out who lies behind the crime. Why a celebrated sculptor should be kidnapped as well though, is more puzzling, and increases the alarm.

The MASK mission: to rescue the kidnapped from VENOM's wicked grasp, and return them safely to their natural homes. With the help of Scott and T-Bob, the MASK agents are called on to combat the EVIL NETWORK OF MAYHEM once again.

Did you know that there are three other exciting MASK adventures?

MASK 1 – THE DEATHSTONE
A meteor, which in the right hands can be the key to a life-saving technique for mankind, but which in the wrong hands can prove a lethal enemy, falls to earth in the rocky desert. When VENOM come by it, and plan to sell pieces of it off as powerful weapons, MASK has a vital mission before it.

MASK 2 – PERIL UNDER PARIS
When MASK discovers that VENOM holds a map of Paris' underground sewage system with some very strange locations marked onto it, they soon realise that a terrible danger threatens the city.

MASK 3 – VENICE MENACE
VENOM leader Miles Mayhem's evil scheme to dominate the world, has brought Venice – the city of canals – to a mysterious halt. But MASK is close at hand.